ORCA
YOUNG
READERS

Golden Eagle
Book Award

TJ and the Rockets

Hazel Hutchins

D1602857

ORCA BOOK PUBLISHERS

Copyright © 2004 Hazel Hutchins

All rights reserved. No part of this publication may be reproduced or transmitted in any form or by any means, electronic or mechanical, including photocopying, recording or by any information storage and retrieval system now known or to be invented, without permission in writing from the publisher.

National Library of Canada Cataloguing in Publication Data

Hutchins, H. J. (Hazel J.)
TJ and the rockets / Hazel Hutchins.

"Orca young reader".
ISBN 1-55143-300-1

I. Title.

PS8565.U826T33 2004   jC813'.54   C2004-901634-2

Library of Congress Control Number: 2004103567

Summary: Can TJ overcome his fear of failure and build a rocket for the upcoming science fair?

Free teachers' guide available.

Orca Book Publishers gratefully acknowledges the support for its publishing programs provided by the following agencies: the Government of Canada through the Book Publishing Industry Development Program (BPIDP), the Canada Council for the Arts, and the British Columbia Arts Council.

Cover design by Lynn O'Rourke
Cover & interior illustrations by Kyrsten Brooker

In Canada:
Orca Book Publishers
1030 North Park Street
Victoria, BC Canada
V8T 1C6

In the United States:
Orca Book Publishers
PO Box 468
Custer, WA   USA
98240-0468

07 06 05 04 • 6 5 4 3 2 1

Printed and bound in Canada
Printed on 100% post-consumer recycled paper,
100% old growth forest free, processed chlorine free
using vegetable, low VOC inks.

To Wil—
who kept life exciting for everyone
with inventions and rocket launches
while he was growing up.
—H.H.

Chapter 1

My name is TJ Barnes and sometimes I should quit while I'm ahead.

Early Thursday morning, Gran turned up at our door with a long, skinny box. Inside were cardboard rolls, balsa wood and knotted string.

"It's a kit I picked up for you at a garage sale, TJ," she said. "Smell this."

She placed a small gray tube in my hand. The smell was sharp and smoky all at once.

"Gunpowder," said Gran.

I couldn't believe what Gran was saying.

"You want me to build a bomb?" I asked.

Gran shook her head "no" and looked totally pleased at the same time.

"Model rockets—the kind that really fly," said Gran. "That's a used rocket engine. The smell really does remind me of gunpowder."

I didn't know what to say. I didn't know anything about model rockets.

"Do you remember telling me that the worst thing about school this year was going to be the science fair?" asked Gran. "I thought this might help."

The science fair—just the mention of it was enough to ruin my day. I didn't mind doing projects in class, but the idea of a science fair, when everyone in the whole school was going to walk by and say, "Look what a dumb thing TJ's come up with," made me feel sick to my stomach. It especially made me feel sick when the person who taught science to the other class was Mr. Wilson.

Mr. Wilson is Mr. Super Science himself. He's built an entire laboratory in the back of his classroom. He has all kinds of special equipment—beakers, batteries, microscopes, chemicals and books about everything under the sun. If you believe the rumors, he practically does the projects *for* the kids—not that anyone ever admits it. Would you admit it if you had the most amazing project ever?

And there's another problem. Ever since I was little, things go wrong, wrong, wrong for me whenever Mr. Wilson is around.

In grade one, on the first really cold day, it was Mr. Wilson who found me with my tongue stuck to the bike rack.

In grade two it was Mr. Wilson who figured out that I was walking funny because I'd Crazy-Glued my fingers to my kneecap.

In grade three it was Mr. Wilson who was standing by the garbage pail in the hall the time I had to be sick and missed the bucket.

I could go on, but I think you get the picture. I guess I must have looked sick again because Gran tried to reassure me, even if she didn't know what I was feeling sick about.

"You can do it all yourself, TJ," she said. "I only have to be there when you launch. There are instructions and safety rules right in the box."

Suddenly there was a thumping noise overhead. We looked up. Neither of us had X-ray vision, but we could guess what was going on.

"Say hi to the wild teenagers for me," Gran said with a grin. "I've got to run."

The next moment Gran was out the door and I was on my way upstairs.

The teenagers were my kittens, Alaska and T-Rex. I'd taken care of Gran's four cats last year and now I had two of my own. They were nine months old and full of the kind of energy that sometimes got them into trouble; that's why Gran called them the wild teenagers.

As I reached the top of the stairs the thumping noise stopped and something small and metal came flying—*smack*—out the bathroom door.

I looked into the bathroom. T-Rex was sitting innocently in the tub. He's gray with little white paddy paws and great big kitten eyes. Those big eyes were looking up and they were very bright and shiny. Hunting eyes.

Clink.

A hairpin fell into the tub. Instantly, T-Rex attacked it. When T-Rex cuffs something around the bathtub, he puts his whole body into it. *Thump, thump, thump, thump—plop.* This time he sent it shooting out of the tub and into the toilet. Yuck! I didn't want to have to fish hairpins out of the toilet!

But T-Rex was sitting innocently, looking up again. I looked up too. There was Alaska, all black and orange and white, sitting on top of the medicine cabinet. She had squeezed in between the shampoo and the hair gel. She was pushing hairpins into the bathtub below.

Clink.

This one landed on the floor instead of in the tub. T-Rex ignored it.

"Be careful," I told Alaska.

There wasn't much room for her between the hair gel and shampoo. She had to keep reaching further and further behind the containers to find the pins. The hair gel gave a little wobble.

"Look out," I told her.

But even I couldn't see what was coming next.

"Alaskaaa!"

When my best friend, Seymour, arrived ten minutes later, I was holding a towel-wrapped kitten under each arm.

"Did you know a single pair of cats can cover an entire bathroom with hair gel?" I asked. "First they push it off a high shelf so that it explodes and then they dance in it."

"Another amazing cat fact," said Seymour.

We'd done a report on cats last year. We were always looking for new facts.

"Does the dance include dressing up like Egyptian mummy-cats?" asked Seymour.

"They looked like a couple of punk rockers a few minutes ago," I said. "I had to get them washed before they started licking themselves. Here, take this."

I handed T-Rex to Seymour for drying. I dried Alaska. We set them on the floor.

Alaska shook one back leg and then the other as if she were doing some sort of disco dance. T-Rex walked around like a high-stepping wet rat. Seymour and I couldn't help it. We laughed so hard our sides hurt. The kittens looked disgusted and went into the living room.

I grabbed my schoolbooks from the table. Seymour pointed to the box that Gran had left.

"What's that?" he asked.

"Gran seems to think it's my science project," I said.

"Looks like a mess to me," said Seymour as we headed out the door. "Did I tell you? I'm not going to do a regular project."

"Everyone has to do a science fair project," I said.

"I'm not," said Seymour. "I'm doing something better."

And that was all I could get out of him because we were late and had to run for it.

Chapter 2

It's like I always say—our teacher, Ms. Kovalski is a witch. She *knows* things.

SCIENCE FAIR!

It was written on the blackboard when we got to school that morning. Not one word about it until now, but as soon as Seymour and I thought about it just the tiniest amount, there she was way ahead of us.

"This is it—the year you get to do the best projects ever and display them in the gym. Has anyone decided what to do?" she asked.

There was a long moment of silence. Then Gabe called from the back of the room. "I've decided to be sick that day!"

Everyone turned to look at him. Gabe is *never* sick. If he were sick, his parents would make him stay home from hockey practice or soccer practice or baseball practice. Gabe hates school, but he loves sports. He doesn't play sick. Ever.

The next moment everyone else started calling out too.

"I'm going to be sick the whole week!" said Jen.

"I'm going to be sick the whole month!" said Roddy.

"I'm going to be sick for the rest of the year!" said Mia.

I hadn't realized that everyone in class felt the way I did. Even Amanda Baker, the smartest kid in the room, was nodding her head.

We all knew what was going to happen. One part of the gym would be full of the amazing projects done by Mr. Wilson's class. The other part of the gym would have the very ordinary, very pathetic-looking attempts done by the kids who didn't have Mr. Wilson for a teacher. We'd all seen it. I guess we'd all secretly assumed, back when we were little, that we'd be the ones in Mr. Wilson's class with the wonderful projects. We weren't. We had Ms. K.

But we liked Ms. K.! We liked her a lot! We had her last year, and everyone asked to be in her class again when she moved up to the next grade. If we could just make the science fair go away, everything would be fine.

Ms. K. took a deep breath and straightened her shoulders.

"I'm sure you'll all come up with excellent projects," she said. "Let's get out our books."

She was acting brave, but everyone could tell that even she was worried. Being a witch and *knowing* things is different from being a scientist and helping someone build a solar-powered radio.

"I told you," I said to Seymour after class. "We all have to be in the science fair. Even being sick for the rest of the year doesn't count."

"I didn't say I wasn't going to be in the science fair," said Seymour. "I just said I wasn't doing a regular project."

"What *are* you doing?" I asked.

"I've got to go to the library first," said Seymour. "I'll tell you at the store later."

The store is my mom and dad's hardware store. It's not a big place, but they've always wanted to run their own business and they're really proud of it.

Thursdays after school and Saturday afternoons I take care of the pet supplies; that's my department. After that I help wherever else I'm needed. I'm not old enough for it to be "officially" a job, but it's pretty much the same except I only do it because I want to. That day a big order had come in, and Mr. G., who started working at the store about two months ago, helped me carry out the boxes.

I like Mr. G. He jokes with everybody while he works. He joked with a carpenter about buying a board stretcher (a board stretcher almost sounds like it might be a real tool—until you think about it). He even got a smile out of a lady with frizzy gray hair and a frizzy gray knitting bag while he sold her a bar of soap.

"Where's your excitable friend today?" asked Mr. G. as he brought out the last of the boxes.

"Living dangerously at the library," I said.

Mr. G. laughed and headed home for the day.

Talking about Seymour made me think about the science fair again. So did seeing Amanda's mom when she came in to buy diet food for their cat. After that I ducked into a side aisle to avoid Mr. Wilson, who walked by with six boxes of batteries that were on sale. Someone in his class was probably going to build a giant electromagnet that could lift small locomotives. How could I *not* think about the science fair?

"TJ, have you seen the radio alarm clock we had, the one with the giant snooze button?"

Mom was standing at the end of the aisle. She was holding her mouth funny, the way she does when something is bugging her, but she wants to pretend it isn't. What was going on?

"Nope," I said. "But I can look for it."

Mom nodded. "Thanks," she said. "I don't remember it going through the till."

I walked around the store to look for the alarm clock. Sometimes customers pick something up and leave it somewhere else. I was in the household section when Seymour showed up. Books stuck out the top of his backpack, and he had a strange look in his eye. Mr. G. thought I was joking about the library being a dangerous place, but in Seymour's case it's true.

"It's an even better idea than I thought!" he announced.

He picked up a flyswatter and began smacking the shelf.

"A schoolteacher invented this a hundred years ago. The little holes let the air pass through. No one's ever invented anything better for swatting flies."

Mom and Dad like Seymour, but they don't like it when he starts being loud in the store. I took away the flyswatter. Seymour picked up a couple of can-openers and began waving them around.

"The first tin cans had to be opened with a chisel and a hammer," said Seymour. "A chisel and hammer! Someone had to *invent* the can-opener!"

I took the can-openers away and steered him into the next aisle.

"The lightbulb!" announced Seymour. "Invented by Thomas Edison, who had a whole *system* of inventing."

He moved a few steps down the aisle.

"Flashlights!" said Seymour. "Did you know that the first flashlights were invented as electric flowerpots?"

I didn't know it, and I didn't believe it either. I figured it was time to head home. I hurried to the back room to grab my jacket. When I came out, Seymour was in the middle of the aisle, waving a pair of gumboots.

"Rubber!" he called across the store. "Usable rubber was invented by accident—by *accident!*"

The toy section was the fastest way to reach the front door.

"Monopoly!" This time Seymour's excitement reached new heights. "Charles Darrow invented it when he was out of work. He became a multimillionaire!"

We'd reached the checkout counter. Happily Mr. Wilson was gone, but a man with a beard was buying nails in a small paper bag.

"Paper bags used to be flat like envelopes," Seymour told him. "A store owner invented bottoms and folding sides. A lady invented a machine to make zillions of them at a time."

The customer looked sideways at Seymour, paid quickly and left the store. The *ping* of the till set Seymour off again.

"The first cash register was invented by a bar owner who wanted to stop his staff from stealing money. He got the idea from a machine that counted how many times a propeller went around!"

I crowded Seymour out the door.

"TJ?" Mom called.

I stuck my head back inside.

"Did you find that alarm clock?"

I shook my head.

"Maybe Mr. G. sold it," I said. "Or maybe Dad's turning it into some kind of marketing gimmick. *Don't Be Alarmed—It's Time to Visit Barnes' Hardware Store.*"

I like it when Mom laughs. Parents who run hardware stores can get way too serious and worried about things.

"Zip up your coat!" she called as I went out the door.

Of course I didn't zip it up, but it set Seymour off again.

"A hundred years ago you wouldn't have been able to zip up your coat because zippers weren't invented," he said.

"A hundred years ago I didn't have a coat to zip up," I told him. "I didn't have fingers to zip with. I didn't have hands to attach fingers to. Now stop with the inventions because I've got it figured out—you're going to invent something for the science fair."

"It's even bigger than that," said Seymour. "Think how neat it will be to have a friend who is a famous inventor. Years and years from now you'll be able to say, 'This invention changed the world, and all because of my friend Seymour'!"

I hate it when Seymour gets that kind of look on his face, mysterious and hopeful all at once. Suddenly, however, his expression changed to a frown.

"But it's got to be a secret," said Seymour. "I don't want Mr. Wilson's class stealing my idea of inventing things and using his fancy equipment."

I nodded. That part I understood. Seymour grinned again.

"So it's a great idea, right?" he asked. "Seymour, the Inventor!"

"I'll ask the kittens what they think," I said.

"Ask T-Rex first," said Seymour. "Tell him I'm the one who's inventing something. And remember to feed him at the same time."

When I got home, however, T-Rex wasn't hungry. Neither was Alaska. I was really, really worried that they were sick. I grew even more worried when they disappeared. Cats who are really sick sometimes go off alone to die. I didn't want the kittens to die!

Suddenly I heard strange noises in

the laundry room. I raced in, thinking I might need to do something heroic to save them.

Nope. The cat-food bag on the top shelf now had a big hole chewed in the corner, and they were feeding themselves by the gravity-flow method.

The wild teenagers had turned into a pair of juvenile delinquents.

Chapter 3

That night, just before I went to bed, I rummaged through the rocket box. Alaska and T-Rex rummaged with me.

"Most engines for model rockets use black powder as a propellant," I read aloud from one of the booklets. Gran was right. These rockets really flew—not into outer space, but definitely up into "bird land" if the diagrams were correct.

"Do you think I could build one?" I asked the cats. "Do you think it would fall apart if Mr. Wilson was around?"

The cats couldn't decide. Neither could I. Every night for the next week we got out the box. We read and rummaged. It was the following Wednesday when

Amanda Baker announced her science project in class.

"Parallax," she said. "That's how humans have estimated how far it is to the planets and the stars."

Amanda never ceases to amaze me. When Ms. K. had mentioned the science fair, Amanda had been as discouraged as the rest of us. A week later she'd come up with an idea that took in the entire universe. And it's not like you can run a tape measure out into the universe.

"Hold your finger way far out in front of your face and close one eye and then the other—your finger will seem to move," said Amanda. "Now hold your finger closer in and do the same thing. Your finger appears to move even more. That's the basis of parallax and it's one way to measure the distance to the stars."

Of course for the next fifteen minutes everybody in class, including Ms. K., was doing weird winking stuff with their fingers and rulers and pencils and anything else they could find.

"Trust Amanda to think of something neat!" said Seymour after school. "Now I'm a million times as glad that I thought of inventing something."

Seymour likes Amanda in his own way—Amanda is not only the smartest kid in class; she's also the nicest kid—but it drives him crazy when she does things better than he does, which is most of the time.

"*Have* you invented something?" I asked.

Amanda was the only one who'd actually told Ms. K. that she had a project.

"I'm not there yet," said Seymour. "The books say there are three stages to inventing—immersion, incubation, illumination. I'm still at stage one. I'm filling my brain with the *idea* of inventing."

When Seymour thinks hard, one eyebrow goes up and one eyebrow goes down and he gets a cross-eyed look.

"Until I started reading the books, I didn't realize how many inventions there are in the world," said Seymour. "They're everywhere."

He pointed to the cars waiting at the street corner.

"Traffic lights are an invention. The first one was a lantern. A policeman stood underneath and turned it back and forth with a lever—red, green, red, green. One day it exploded. Someone had to invent a better one."

The light changed. The traffic came toward us. I thought he'd say that cars were an invention. Instead he was staring at the tires.

"Inflatable tires," he said. "The Michelin brothers were the first people to make tires with air in them. They took 22 inner tubes on a car race in France and had so many flat tires they used them all."

He was right. Cars were an invention, but so were all the parts that went into a car. I hadn't thought about that before.

We were walking by a store that sold furniture. A rug was hanging in the window.

"The game of Parcheesi was invented by workers making rugs in India. They played it on the pattern they were weaving," said Seymour. "Akbar the Great had a giant Parcheesi board made in his garden with colored tiles and real live people as playing pieces."

Seymour really did know lots of neat things about inventions.

"So what are you going to invent?" I asked.

"It's like I told you," said Seymour. "I'm just at the first stage. Immersion."

In other words he didn't have the faintest idea.

"You could help me," he said. "We could both be great inventors!"

Sometimes I like doing projects with Seymour. Other times he drives me crazy. At that moment I came to my decision—kind of.

"I'm going to build something from the box Gran gave me," I said.

"You're going to build a mess for a science project?" he asked.

"A model rocket," I said. "But you can't blab about it until I'm sure I can build one that really works and doesn't fall apart the minute Mr. Wilson shows up."

24

"Good plan," said Seymour. "Do you remember the time you barfed all over his shoes? And the time you crashed into his car with your bike?"

I'd forgotten about the crash.

"There's a rocket already built that needs repairing. I'm going to try that first," I said.

"Is there any science to it?" asked Seymour. "Are you sure it isn't just some kind of pop-up toy?"

"There's all kinds of science—force and thrust and Newton's laws of motion," I said. "The engines use a chemical reaction like fireworks."

"Fireworks and gunpowder were invented by the Chinese," said Seymour. "Dynamite was later. The guy who started the Nobel Peace Prize invented dynamite. That was his name—Nobel. He didn't want dynamite used for war, just for things like building roads and tunnels."

Seymour looked at me thoughtfully.

"When you get around to launching, let me know so I can watch," he said.

"Maybe it'll give me an idea about something to invent."

That night, the kittens changed from rummaging to doing a little inventing of their own. T-Rex invented a game called "Run Around with a Plastic Parachute on Your Head." I don't think it will be as popular as Monopoly.

Alaska invented cement overshoes. That's what happens when a cat walks through glue and then decides to use the kitty litter. At least this time I only had to wash her feet.

In between the cats' inventions, I worked on the rocket. It was about as long as the two kittens. I cut two fins from balsa wood and glued them in place where the original ones had broken away. I found a nose cone that fit, strung a parachute for it and connected the sections together with shock cord. One more night to repaint and it would be ready.

Gran phoned just as I was putting things away.

"Is Saturday morning a good time to launch?" she asked.

Gran is like Seymour. She doesn't waste time with "Hello, how are you?"

"How do you know I built one?" I asked.

Gran laughed. "I don't," she said. "Did you?"

"Saturday would be great," I said.

I made sure I put everything away before Mom and Dad got home. They work hard thinking about the store, and I didn't want them to have to think about my science project. I needn't have worried. When they got home they were totally distracted. Dad was frowning so hard his forehead looked like it had tire tracks across it, both the inflatable and the solid kind.

"TJ, did you see anyone eying that drill I had out on display last Saturday?"

"Did someone break it?" I asked.

"Nope," said Dad. "It took a walk."

"Took a walk" is what Dad calls it when something gets stolen from the store. I remembered the alarm clock Mom asked me about last week. I looked at her. She nodded.

"It's been getting bad lately," she said.

"I think we should look into a security system," said Dad. "What about that salesman who was in a few days ago and wanted to show us one?"

"He said he'd be back this week," said Mom. "But it's bound to cost a lot. And a lot of our customers like us because we're a friendly neighborhood store."

"I know," said Dad and frowned even harder.

After that they didn't talk about it anymore. In fact, they tried really hard not to talk about it. That's how they get when something's really bothering them.

It really bothered me too. It makes me mad when people steal things. I know it happens in every business, but when it's your store and you know a bit about how businesses have to pay rent, light, heat, cleaning and bank loans and then try to take out wages too so that you can actually eat that month, it begins to feel a whole lot more personal.

I was still thinking about it as I got ready for bed. That's when the phone rang.

"The number zero!"

It was Seymour. Who else would it be?

"Think of it, TJ, the number zero is an invention!"

"No it's not," I said. "You can't invent a nothing. It's always *not* there."

"But there hasn't always been a number for it," said Seymour. "And it does other things too. It lines up numbers so you can add them. It turns 1 into 10. An Arab mathematician brought it to Europe in the eighth century. Without zero there wouldn't be modern mathematics."

"Seymour," I said, "you hate mathematics."

"Maybe I could invent something like zero only different that would make kids like math!" said Seymour.

I figured he was already asleep and dreaming.

Chapter 4

Saturday morning was clear and calm. It was perfect weather for launching a model rocket.

"Ten...nine..."

Gran had driven us to an open area at the edge of the city. She'd gone over the safety rules with Seymour and me, and then she'd settled in a lawn chair by the car. We'd walked to the middle of the field to set up.

"Eight...seven..."

Our only audience was a herd of cows beyond a barbed wire fence. I wouldn't have noticed the cows, but Seymour had pointed them out. That's also when he'd stepped on one of the rocket's fins. Luckily it had only been a tiny bit loose and I'd fixed it with duct tape.

"Six...five..."

We were standing back the required distance. Seymour was doing the countdown. I had the ignition button in my hand.

"Four...three..."

I couldn't help but feel excited. The paint job had turned out better than I'd expected. Standing upright on the launchpad, the rocket looked almost real in a miniature sort of way. It looked as if it actually wanted to fly.

"Two..."

A wonderful tingle sped down my spine.

"One..."

I took a deep breath.

"Blast off!" cried Seymour.

I pressed the ignition button.

Woooosh! The rocket shot into the air. Boy did it go! I was amazed.

Vssssssss. The sound changed as it started to wobble.

Swoo-swoo-swoo-swooo. The rocket was arching over. It was way above the ground, so it wasn't dangerous, but it wasn't going up the way it was supposed to go. It was going sideways, and it was spinning like crazy.

"Oh no!" shouted Seymour. "The cows!"

The next moment everything changed. We heard a pop—a second mini "explosion" that was part of the engine's timing. The nose cone popped off. The parachute appeared. It was supposed to spread wide and drift the rocket safely back to earth.

That wasn't what was happening. It all just kept going sideways and spinning. The strings were wrapping around the parachute, and the parachute was wrapping around the rocket. What a mess.

All of a sudden I noticed a stand of trees along one end of the fence. I hadn't even seen them there before. The rocket was heading straight for them.

"No!" I cried.

Seymour and I ran as hard and fast as we could, but it was hopeless. Somewhere in the matted tops of the trees, the rocket came to rest. All we could do was stand there with our necks craned back.

"And you were worried about the cows getting hurt," I said.

"I wasn't worried about them," said Seymour. "I was worried because they might have gone crazy and trampled the rocket. That's what a bunch of peasants did to one of the early balloon flights. They thought they were being invaded by creatures from another planet and hacked the balloon to pieces."

I sighed. "It might just as well have got trampled by cows," I said. "I'm not going to get it back."

We walked back across the field to collect the launchpad and other gear. Why was I so disappointed? It's not like it was really my science project. It's not like I'd expected it to work.

But it had worked! It had lifted off perfectly. What had gone wrong?

"Tough luck, TJ," said Gran.

I nodded, but I knew luck didn't have anything to do with it. *Something* had gone wrong. What was it? Could Mr.

Wilson jinx my science project even when he wasn't here? And why did I care?

The whole thing was really, really bugging me. It was bugging me more than I'd thought it would. It wasn't just the work I'd put into the rocket. It was the excitement of the launch itself.

Just before we climbed into the car, Seymour stopped and looked back at the trees. One eyebrow went up and one eyebrow went down.

"Maybe I could invent something for people to get their rockets back from the treetops," he said.

Gran dropped Seymour and me off at the store. Seymour wandered around for a while then headed home. I tried to forget about the rocket launch. The store was busy and I knew it was one of those times when someone might try to shoplift.

I did my best to keep an eye on every-one who came through the door, but it was pretty much impossible. After a while I couldn't remember them all, let alone watch them. I jotted down notes on the lid of a cardboard box about who had been in.

Amanda's mother returned the cat food. Her cat wouldn't eat it and the supplier guaranteed satisfaction or money back. I guess the Baker family was going to have a happy fat cat instead of a crabby skinny one.

After that the list contained things like "guy with beard, two teenagers with portable CD players, soap lady with frizzy hair, waiter from restaurant across street, six little kids and mother with wild expression."

Mr. G. liked the store even better when there were lots of people around. He just kept joking with everyone, including his carpenter friend.

"I hear you've been cutting boards twice and they're still too short," he said.

"I hear you've been hammering nails and blaming the wind for bending them over," the carpenter joked right back.

I was so busy listening to them banter back and forth that I turned around and walked—*smack*—into a post.

"Careful, TJ."

I knew who it was before I even opened my eyes. Mr. Wilson.

"Ahh, can I help you?" I asked.

"Actually, you can," said Mr. Wilson. "Since I've run into you, or rather since you've run into that post, I wanted to ask you something. How is your class making out with its science fair projects? I know Ms. K. hasn't done the science fair before, and I'm a little concerned."

I felt my face go even redder. It was one thing for him to be my own personal jinx; it was another thing for him to be checking up on Ms. K.! I leapt instantly to her defense without caring whether or not what I said was true.

"We're doing great," I said. "She's a great teacher. She can teach anything, especially science. We've got all kinds of neat projects. Even Gabe has a great project, and you know how much Gabe hates school."

Mr. Wilson broke into a broad grin.

"Excellent! I have to go out of town,

and this might work out even better than I thought," he said and walked happily away.

Which left me wondering what I'd done.

Chapter 5

On Monday morning, Ms. K. had an announcement to make.

"Mr. Wilson has moved the science fair ahead," she said as she wrote the new date on the board. It was only two weeks away!

"Doesn't matter to me!" called out Gabe from the back of the room. "I can be sick that week just as well as any other!"

"No one is going to be sick," said Ms. K. "And I'd like you to bring in your collections tomorrow."

"We don't do collections this year," said Amanda.

"We already did collections back in grade three," said Roddy.

"If we start looking at everyone's collections, we won't have time to think about our science projects!" said Mia.

"Exactly," said Ms. K. "It's something we can do for fun instead of going crazy over this science fair business. Please bring in your collections tomorrow."

"It's all my fault," I told Ms. K. after class. "Mr. Wilson asked me about the science fair, so I told him we all had amazing projects and we were practically finished."

Ms. K. just kept smiling her witchy smile.

"I gathered that when I spoke with him this morning," she said. "But frankly, TJ, it doesn't matter. What difference does it make if the science fair is a month from now or two weeks from now? No one, except Amanda, has even tried to think up an idea. And no one, including Amanda, really gets down to work until about a week before any project is due."

It wasn't quite true. Seymour and I had been thinking about the science fair, even if we hadn't told anyone else about it. Hey—maybe everyone had secret science fair projects and we were all about to amaze ourselves!

Fat chance.

I still thought Ms. K. was crazy not to be working on science fair stuff. Seymour thought so too.

"I've reached stage two," he announced after school. "Incubation. I'm thinking up lots of ideas and writing them down right away so they don't get lost. That's what this notebook is for. And a book like this is important when you go to register a patent so no one can steal your invention."

"Seymour, kids don't invent the kind of things that need patents," I said.

"What about earmuffs?" said Seymour. "Chester Greenwood was only fifteen when he invented them. He had the kind of ears that turned blue when he tried out his new hockey skates on the pond and he hated wool toques. He invented earmuffs. It was the beginning of a whole lifetime of inventing and patents."

"Fifteen is a teenager not a kid," I said.

41

"Close enough," said Seymour. "And what about the kid who invented the Popsicle? He was eleven years old. I'm eleven years old! Frank Epperson—that was his name. At first he called it the Epsicle."

"Are you sure?" I asked.

"I'm sure!" said Seymour. "The trampoline was invented by a guy who used to jump up and down on the bed in the guest room when he was just a kid. The idea of colored car wax to cover scratches was invented by some girl who was twelve years old."

He rapped on the notebook.

"It's hardcover so it can't be destroyed easily. It has pages that don't pull out. There's no place to add extra pages either. That's important. I'm writing on every line so no one can claim I added something in later, and I'm writing in pen and I'm dating it and you're going to sign it every day.

"Why am I going to sign it?"

"To prove I invented it before anyone else."

I looked at the first page. So far he had invented his name and address.

"I know, I know," he said. "I haven't quite got started. That's why I thought I'd walk you home. Your house is a good place for coming up with ideas."

Well it was a good place for the cats to come up with ideas. They'd come up with a lot of them lately. Mostly they were the kind of ideas that knocked things over or tore things apart. However Alaska also had another trick.

"Is she there?" I called.

I'd sent Seymour half a block ahead. Every time I came home, no matter what time of day it was, I always found Alaska sitting in the window looking out at me. She wasn't there when Dad or Mom came home. She wasn't there when the mailman came by or when Gran dropped over—I'd asked them. But somehow she knew when I was coming. I wanted to see if the way she knew was by spotting me coming down the street.

"She's already here," called Seymour. "Green-eyed fur face at two o'clock."

Sure enough, when I got to our gate, there was Alaska looking out. How did she do that?

As usual she watched us come up the walk, but when we reached the bottom step her face vanished from the window. I handed Seymour the front-door key.

"You go first," I said.

"Is this another cat thing?" he asked.

I nodded.

Seymour opened the door and went inside.

"Hello!" he called. "Alaska! T-Rex!"

Not a cat in sight. Seymour shrugged and bent over to undo his runners.

Tha-da–da-thump—wham!

A gray blur came barreling down the stairs, threw itself against his shoes and hands and took off again.

"Wow! Was that T-Rex or a jet plane?" Seymour said. "When did he start doing that?"

"Sometime last week," I said. "He seems to be getting better at it. Or worse."

"That's the fastest thirty-one kilometers an hour I've ever seen," said Seymour.

Thirty-one kilometers an hour is top speed for a house cat.

Two seconds later, T-Rex was back, mewing and purring and all friendly. He rubbed himself back and forth against Seymour's ankles and wove in and around my legs. He was marking us with his scent glands. Mine. Mine. Mine. If they ever make infrared goggles that pick up cat scent, my legs are going to positively glow in the dark.

"We'd better find Alaska right away," I said.

Seymour looked puzzled, but he followed me around the house. We found her on a shelf above the desk. She was sitting between a stack of books and a plastic cup full of pens. She was rubbing her furry face against the cup. It was moving closer to the brink and tipping, tipping, going, going...

The pens spilled across the carpet. Alaska peered down at us as we crawled on our hands and knees to pick them up. I think she was laughing, but it's hard to tell with a cat.

I lifted her down before we went into the kitchen. Seymour crumpled a couple of pieces of scrap paper into balls and threw them around the floor to keep the cats busy while I made us a snack. After that I filled their food dishes to keep them out of our faces while we were eating.

Seymour took out his notebook and spread it on the table. He stared at it.

"Are you sure that's what they mean by incubation? Staring at a blank page?"

"I'm not staring," said Seymour. "I'm thinking."

"Looks pretty much like staring to me."

T-Rex seemed to feel the same way. He gobbled the last of his crunchies, jumped onto the table beside Seymour and stared at the book too. He wasn't supposed to be on the table, but Mom wasn't home and I think he looks cute up there. Seymour looked across to see a "cat image" of himself staring at a blank page.

"Maybe you're right," said Seymour. "I need inspiration. I need to think big like ...like...Leonardo da Vinci."

"I thought he painted the *Mona Lisa*," I said.

"He did," said Seymour. "But he was an inventor too. He patented all sorts of inventions, even way back then. He watched birds and came up with plans for flying machines. He watched fish swim and drew plans for submarines. They didn't actually work, but he was on the right track."

Seymour scratched his head. Now his hair was standing up even more than usual. He actually looked the part of a mad inventor.

"Come to think of it, other inventors have got their ideas from nature too," said Seymour. "The idea for hot air balloons came from two brothers watching pieces of paper rise on the hot air above their factory. And Velcro—you know that sticky kind of cloth? Velcro was invented by a Swiss engineer who found cockleburs clinging to his jacket."

Seymour took his snack into the living room. For the next ten minutes, instead of staring at a blank page on our kitchen table, he stared out the window at our yard. I sat on the living room sofa and read through some of the rocket-building instructions I'd dug out of the bottom of the box. I was about halfway through the pages when I found some interesting information.

The fin is the stabilizing and guiding unit of a model rocket. When a rocket is momentarily deflected by even a small gust of wind, the fins enable it to correct the flight and fly straight again.

Aha! Illumination, as Seymour would say. The loose fin—that's what had gone wrong with my rocket. I'd thought duct tape would hold it, but I hadn't realized the kind of force that a launch would involve.

Seymour had finished his snack and was headed back into the kitchen.

"Any luck?" I asked him.

"Naw," said Seymour. "God already invented trees. Did a pretty good job too."

That's when we heard the noise. *Lap lap lap.*

I followed Seymour into the kitchen. T-Rex had knocked over Seymour's half-full glass of milk. He was busy cleaning up the evidence.

What really made us stop and stare, however, was Alaska. Alaska was sitting by my own glass of milk. She hadn't knocked it over, and she wasn't sticking her head inside either. Instead she was reaching into the glass with her lovely little paddy paw, delicately scooping out milk and daintily licking.

"Hey!" said Seymour. "Alaska just invented the spoon!"

Which was true, cat-style at least.

Chapter 6

It was Tuesday when Dad noticed that one of the expensive Swiss Army knives was missing from the lockup case.

"Not again," said Mom.

"It was there on Saturday," I said. "Mr. G. opened the case so Seymour could look at it. Seymour's on an invention kick, and he thought it was pretty neat."

Dad nodded.

"So it was stolen sometime between Saturday at noon and noon today," he said. "Maybe Wilf left the case open by mistake."

Wilf Grogan is Mr. G.'s real name.

"He might have," I said. "He had to help a couple of other customers while Seymour was looking at it."

"You've got a good memory, TJ," said Mom.

"I was trying to watch who was in the store," I said. "If I ever catch the person who's stealing stuff, they're really going to be sorry."

"Watch all you like, but don't go chasing after them," said Dad. "You never know what a person will do, and we don't want anyone getting hurt. Tell me or Mom or Mr. G. if you suspect someone."

That's what parents always say.

The next morning, Seymour and I took a detour when we got to school. We walked past Mr. Wilson's room. Through the door we could glimpse what looked like an entire ocean of science projects— giant springs, long glass tubing, boards with electric wires, switches and light-bulbs.

Our own room looked pretty much as usual—messy. Witches tend to have all sorts of different things lying around, and since kids had been bringing in their collections, it was worse than usual.

The last person to bring in a collection was Gabe. He'd asked for an extra day to get organized. Since when did Gabe get anything organized except on the playing field?

But when he arrived with his sports cards, everyone was surprised. The cards were all in plastic pages; the pages were tabbed and sorted into binders; the binders looked as if they had never been touched by unwashed hands.

"I buy them with my paper-route money," he said. "Most of what I earn has to go to hockey and baseball fees, but I save a little out for cards and it kind of adds up."

"I've never really looked at sports cards before," said Ms. K. "Look at this. It says that this player's pitch has been clocked at ninety three miles an hour. What do they mean 'clocked at'?"

"They aim a gun at it," said Gabe.

"A gun?"

"A kind of a gun that measures speed. You see it in the stands when the scouts are out."

"But how does it work? Is it like the radar guns the police use?"

"I don't know. I've never thought about it."

"Hmmm," said Ms. K. "That makes me wonder something else. Is there a reason these athletes are so good? Is there a reason they can throw so hard? Or shoot a puck accurately? Is it because they try harder? Or have better equipment? Or because of the type of body they have— their muscle mass and their vision and things like that?"

"I don't know," said Gabe. "They're just good."

But you could tell from the look on his face that he had begun to wonder himself.

Mia had a collection of matchbooks. Ms. K. was interested in the places they'd come from. She also wondered if anyone knew how safety matches worked.

"I know, I know, I know!" called Seymour.

"Don't tell us, Seymour, but do tell us one thing. Is there anything scientific about matches?"

I could tell there must be quite a story behind matches because Seymour was just about to burst. He controlled himself, however.

"Lots of science," he said. "Chemistry. Physics. Invention."

It didn't take long until we figured it out, of course. Ms. K. knew she couldn't beat Mr. Wilson in terms of laboratory experiments, so she'd done it from a different angle. She was helping us to find the science in the everyday, the ordinary things that appealed to each of us.

"Proving, once and for all, she's a witch," said Seymour. "Witches don't need special equipment. They just use what's lying around, frogs and toads and stuff like that."

Of course it didn't work for everyone. Some kids didn't really have collections or weren't interested in them the way Gabe was, but it did get everyone thinking that maybe, just maybe, it was possible to do a science project after all.

"I wish she'd let me tell people about safety matches," said Seymour. "It's a neat story. Some guy was trying to invent a new type of explosive. He stirred the chemicals with a stick, and a glob dried on the stick. He tried to get the glob off by rubbing the stick against the stone floor of his shop. Poof. It burst into flame."

"You mean he discovered it by accident?" I asked.

"Yup," said Seymour.

"And was rubber really discovered by accident?" I asked.

Seymour nodded.

"It wasn't completely an accident," he said. "Mr. Goodyear—as in the tire guy—was doing experiments to find ways to keep rubber soft so people could use it. He was already mixing it with chemicals, but he didn't know that heat was going to be the answer until a blob fell accidentally on the stove."

Seymour's eyebrows began to separate. One went up, one went down.

"But safety glass was an accident," he said thoughtfully. "A glass container fell to the floor and shattered, but someone noticed that the pieces still hung together.

It had held liquid plastic once upon a time."

A dreamy tone came into his voice.

"And Ivory Soap was an accident—not the soap itself, but the fact that it floats, which is why people all of a sudden wanted to buy it."

He kept going.

"And Scotchgard was an accident—a scientist dropped some chemical on her tennis shoe and noticed later that the spot never got dirty.

"And cornflakes were an accident—that was the Kellog brothers and their three-day-old mixture that they didn't throw out.

"And chocolate chip cookies were an accident because someone didn't realize that bakers chocolate melts in cookie dough, but a broken-up chocolate bar just stays in nice yummy chunks.

"And Coca-Cola was an accident..."

"Seymour, come back, Seymour," I said. I was waving a hand in front of his face.

"Nope, can't stop yet," said Seymour.

"I'm saving the best for last. Some guy named Fleming accidentally left an experiment with bacteria sitting on a window-sill. It went moldy, but this Fleming guy was smart enough to look at it anyway. He saw that the mold had actually started to dissolve the bacteria. Ta-da! Penicillin."

Which was pretty amazing because even I knew that penicillin was a really important drug. I also had a strong suspicion where Seymour was going with all this.

"Please tell me you're not going to leave a bunch of food lying around," I said.

"Not lying around," said Seymour, "but it is true that a bunch of accidental experiments have to do with food. Are your parents staying late at the store tonight?"

Chapter 7

"What are you and Seymour working on?"

That's what Amanda, smartest kid in class, asked me the next morning.

"How do you know we're working on anything?" I asked.

"I can tell," said Amanda. "First Seymour acts as if he's got the greatest idea in the world. The next day he's going around scowling. That's how he gets when you two are working on a project together. Besides, his hands are purple."

It was true. Last night had not been a great success. Seymour had invented burnt peanut butter, but he couldn't find a use for it. He'd invented stretched marshmallow raisin balls, but they took about three hours to chew. He'd invented health food made with squished tinned beets and oatmeal, but it tasted disgusting and he still couldn't get the color from his hands.

The cats had invented things too.

T-Rex had invented throwing up in the middle of the kitchen table. That was after he ate a bunch of peanut butter when Seymour wasn't looking. Maybe Mom was right about the kittens not sitting on the table.

Alaska had invented a game called "High-Risk Obstacle Course." She jumped on top of the china cabinet and walked between Mom's special glass figurines. I didn't think she could push them off, but then I hadn't thought she could topple the hair gel either. I bribed her down with cat treats and gave her a long talking-to. I'm not entirely sure she was listening.

I was the only one who made any real progress. I'd worked on a new rocket, just a little one this time. It was one kitten length instead of two, and I was going to make sure Seymour didn't step on it.

Amanda was still waiting for my answer.

"I'm not allowed to say. You know how Seymour is. You might out-dinosaur him or out-haunted-house him."

I was talking about a couple of other projects our class had worked on.

"I can't *not* do a good job on something just to make him feel better," said Amanda.

"Why not?" I asked. "It would make my life a whole lot easier."

The look on Amanda's face scared me for a moment.

"I'm joking, Amanda. I really am. Seymour would be totally disgusted if you did something like that. So would I. It's bad enough that we have to go against Mr. Wilson's class. If the smartest kid in our class starts acting weird, then we'll know we're really in trouble."

"I'm only smart in some ways," said Amanda. "There's lots of ways to be smart."

There *are* lots of ways to be smart. I sure wish Seymour would figure out just one of them. Burnt peanut butter smells awful.

It was Thursday, and after school Seymour followed me to the store.

"I've got a new great idea," said Seymour. "Another way people invent things is to take ordinary things and find new uses. Your store is full of ordinary things."

"Take the ice-cream cone," he said, picking up an ice-cream scoop on our way through housewares. "A teenager at the 1904 St. Louis World Fair was selling ice cream in dishes. Right next door was a man selling waffles, a Persian kind of waffle that's really thin. When the dishes ran out, they used rolled-up waffles. Presto—ice-cream cones."

"I didn't know that," said a voice behind us.

"Hey, Mr. G.!" said Seymour.

"Hi, guys," said Mr. G. "Your dad's in the back talking to that slick security salesman, TJ. I'm just going to let your mom know I'm on my way home."

He was carrying his jacket, but he didn't seem to be in a hurry. He leaned back and listened to Seymour talk about inventions.

"Frisbees started out as pie plates," said Seymour. "A company that baked and delivered pies noticed that its customers were throwing the plates around for fun. Hair dryers came from women switching the hoses on their vacuums from the vacuuming-in side to the air-blowing-out side. Liquid Paper started out as plain old white paint. Slinky was a torsion spring from World War II. Tea bags were meant just as packaging, but people dropped the whole thing in their teapots and thought it was great."

Sometimes I don't know whether to believe Seymour or not.

"It's true!" he said. "Look it up yourself."

"I always thought Slinky must have been some sort of happy accident," said Mr. G. "Well, I'd better be off."

We said goodbye to Mr. G. Seymour picked up the closest object on the shelf.

"Take this thing with the holes in it...you could use it...you could use it to put something wet inside and let the water drip out."

"That's what it's for," I said. "It's a strainer."

"Oh," said Seymour. "Well, it could also be..." He turned it over. He turned it sideways. "It could also be..."

"Yes?" I asked.

"Not a good example," said Seymour.

He looked around again.

"Clothespins," he said. "They could be used to hold bags closed or papers together."

I took him around the corner. There on a shelf were all sorts of clamp-type things, not exactly like clothespins but very, very close. They were being used for exactly what Seymour had suggested.

"This plastic tablecloth," said Seymour. Once he gets started, Seymour is not easily discouraged. "This would make a good cover in the rain. Use this broom to hold it up."

"Seymour," I said, "I might be wrong, but I think you just invented the umbrella."

Seymour frowned and put everything back where it had been.

"Everything's already been invented," he sighed. "Everything except stuff like proton separators and anti-gravity machines and stuff you have to go to university for. I haven't got time for university right now."

Seymour went home. I suddenly realized that I hadn't been watching for shoplifters. How could I have forgotten? It was important!

But it wasn't until two days later that I realized how important it was really going to be.

Chapter 8

"TJ, you didn't happen to..." said my mom. I didn't need to wait for the end of the sentence.

It was Saturday morning. Dad had gone to the store early. Mom had some things to do around the house before she left. I was waiting to go rocket flying with Gran and Seymour.

"What was stolen this time?" I asked.

"One of those nice wooden chess sets we brought in."

"Who could be doing it?" I asked.

"At first your dad and I thought it was a couple of kids messing around, you know those two guys who come in with earphones and music so loud they can't hear anyone else?"

The first people everyone suspects are kids. When I go into the corner grocery store, the man who owns it practically stands on top of me. I don't steal things. It drives me nuts when people always think it's kids.

"It's not them, though, is it?"

"I don't think so," said Mom. "They haven't been in all week."

"Who has been in?" I asked.

"All sorts of people," said Mom. "Too many to keep track of. Except that, and I can't be absolutely sure, but the days when things often seem to go missing and I notice they've gone missing are Thursdays and Saturdays."

"Wait a minute!" I said. "Those are the days I'm in the store."

"And the days Seymour drops by," said Mom gently.

I couldn't believe it. She couldn't be saying what I thought she was saying.

"It's not Seymour!" I said. "Seymour's not a thief."

"I didn't say that he was," said my mom.

"You practically did!" Now I was really

mad. "Everyone always blames kids. It doesn't matter if there's a reason or not!"

"I just thought I should mention it," said Mom. "You know that I like Seymour, and usually I trust him, but he's acting weird lately, even for Seymour. Maybe there's something going on that we don't know about. He's always got a packsack and lately he roams up and down the aisles picking up stuff."

"It's not Seymour!" I said. "You were in the store, maybe you stole the stuff if that's all you're going on..."

"TJ..."

I was way too mad to listen. I was so mad I grabbed my rocket gear and went out to wait on the sidewalk for Gran. Luckily she drove up about a minute later.

"What's wrong, TJ?" she asked.

"Everything," I said.

"That about covers it," said Gran.

We picked up Seymour and arrived at Rocket Flats. That's what Seymour and I had nicknamed the field at the edge of town.

"Looks like the cows are delighted to see us again," said Seymour.

"What's with you and cows?" I said.

"I like cows. They just kind of stand there and look peaceful," said Seymour. He frowned. "What are you crabby about? You're the one with the science fair project. I still haven't got an invention."

"I haven't got a science fair project if it flies like last time," I said.

Now that I realized how fast the rocket went, I was extra careful to follow the safety rules. I made sure the fins weren't damaged. I made sure the wind hadn't started to blow, not just down on the ground, but also up where the clouds were.

The most important thing, of course, was to always make sure the ignition key was in my pocket. That way the rocket could never be set off accidentally while Seymour and I were standing close to it.

I put the engine in the rocket, slid it down the launch rod and connected the igniter wires. It really was a little rocket, not even knee high.

"It's cute," said Seymour, stepping back from the launchpad once everything was set up. "I wonder how it will fly."

I was wondering the same thing. Because it was a lot smaller and lighter than the one last time, did that mean it would travel faster? Or would it be slower because the engine also wasn't as power-ful? Would it go as high?

I nodded to Seymour.

"Five, four, three, two, one...liftoff!"

Zing!

Faster than thought the little rocket was in the air and speeding skyward. Up and up. Higher and higher. In no time at all its slender body was only a black speck in the blue. Wow!

Of course as fast as it went up, in the blink of an eye it was also slowing down. Maximum height. Arcing over.

"Streamer time," I said.

I'd been counting under my breath. I knew from the size of engine exactly how many seconds until the second little explosion that would pop the nose cone and release the streamer. The rocket was so light this time that it didn't need a full parachute; just a few plastic streamers would slow it down more than enough.

"Come on, streamers," I said.

The rocket gave a quick shudder, but the nose cone didn't seem to be free. The streamers hadn't appeared.

Faster and faster the rocket dropped, a little dart streaking toward earth.

"The rock pile!" said Seymour.

Why didn't I notice these things ahead of time—the trees, the rock pile? I only really saw they were there when my rocket was headed straight for them.

"No!" I cried.

Smack.

The little rocket landed hard upon the rocks. Seymour and I scrambled up the pile. There it lay—crumpled. The nose cone was only half popped and there were bits of black melted *something* around the outside.

What had happened? Why hadn't the nose cone popped properly? What was the black material plastered on the side?

"The cows were amazed," said Seymour.

I scowled at him, but I managed not to say anything. I *was* crabby and I knew why. It wasn't just the rocket.

As we gathered things up and made our way back to Gran and the car, I could feel my mind jumbling its way through all sorts of things. The worst part about Mom accusing Seymour of stealing was that even though I *knew* it wasn't him, at the back of my mind I was turning it all over and over in my head. I couldn't help myself. I kept looking for times he might have stolen things or reasons he might have taken things. How could I even think that about my best friend?

There was only one solution. I had to figure out who was really taking things. Until I did, I had to keep Seymour away from the store so Mom and Dad wouldn't suspect him anymore.

"I guess we both just have to keep trying," said Seymour as Gran drove us away from the field. "I'm thinking of doing a Rube Goldberg."

"A what?" I asked.

"A Rube Goldberg invention," said Seymour. "They're a kind of super-complicated machine for doing something simple like buttering toast."

I had seen pictures. They seemed more like an un-invention than an invention. I didn't say that to Seymour.

"Sounds great," I said. "Gran can drop you off at home so you can get started."

Seymour shook his head.

"I'll come to the store with you and look around some more. Did you know that creative ideas often come at the spot between waking and sleeping? I'll watch you stock shelves. That's boring enough to put me to sleep."

I definitely didn't want him in the store.

"It's busy in the store on Saturdays, Seymour," I said. "Mom and Dad don't want you falling into a trance in the middle of the place."

"Then we could play mind games, word games. That kind of thinking shakes up your brain and helps you invent things. Look. What's this?"

He picked up the pen and pad Gran kept in the car and wrote

<u>BLACK</u>

COAT

I didn't have the faintest idea. We stopped at a streetlight. Gran glanced at the paper.

"Black overcoat," she said.

"Hey, you're brilliant!" said Seymour. "Maybe you should be the inventor!"

Gran smiled.

"Can you figure out a way to make a quarter go through a hole the size of a penny?" asked Seymour. "Inventors need to visualize the solution even before they try it. We'll practice at the store."

I had to think of something fast.

"Seymour," I said, "necessity is the mother of invention."

Seymour looked at me. One eyebrow went up and one eyebrow went down.

"Thomas Alva Edison," he said.

"Is that who said it?" I asked.

"I don't know," said Seymour. "But his first rule was 'Never invent something that isn't needed.' I forgot about that. And he was one of the greatest!"

"So follow his advice," I said. "Go home and find a problem that needs solving and *then* you'll know what to invent."

I must have made a better argument than I thought because he actually asked to be dropped off at his house.

When I got to the store, Mr. G. was the only one in the front. Dad and Mom were in the storeroom. They were both talking to the security system man this time.

"Are you going to buy it?" I asked when they came out.

"It's a lot of money," said Mom.

"We're going to think about it for a few days longer, but we'll probably go ahead," said my dad.

If they did buy it, everyone would know the store was equipped with it and the stealing would stop. I'd never get a chance to prove it wasn't Seymour!

I really, really kept my eyes peeled that afternoon. The man with a beard was in. So were the plugged-in teenagers. There were some people who looked like they were painting a house, and the man I knew was a carpenter and dozens of other people.

Mr. Wilson came in. I was kind of hoping it was Mr. Wilson, but I followed him around and confirmed what I pretty much suspected. He might be a science nut, but he didn't shoplift.

"Are you following me around, TJ?" asked Mr. Wilson. "Is there something you wanted to talk to me about?"

If I'd had the nerve I would have suggested he help us out with our science projects or at least let his students do their own. I didn't have the nerve.

"You were right about Gabe's project," said Mr. Wilson. "It's a good one."

How did he know what Gabe was doing? I turned back to ask him and— *ka-wham*—knocked over the entire garden seed display. Seed packages flew everywhere.

While I was picking them up, Amanda's mother came into the store. Her cat-food refund was waiting for her and she didn't steal anything. You know you're really desperate when you watch Amanda's mother for shoplifting.

The lady with the frizzy gray hair was in to pick up a bar of soap as she always did. She even smiled and said hello, which at least made me feel a bit better about crawling around on the floor after a bunch of carrot seeds.

It wasn't until I was about to head home that I noticed something. Mom and Dad had put up a schedule at the back of the store to show when everyone was working. I was written down for Thursday and Saturday. Someone else was down for the same days. He worked a few other days too, but the truth was, if you went by the days things were taken, it still fit.

That person was Mr. G.

Chapter 9

Mr. G.! I liked Mr. G. He worked for the store!

Part of me felt sick to my stomach. Part of me was really, really mad. I'd heard on the news that some employees steal from their workplace. How much *had* he stolen?

I didn't tell Mom and Dad. If a kid is accused of shoplifting, everybody believes it. If an adult is accused of shoplifting, you have to have proof. I had to think of a way to prove to Mom and Dad that Mr. G. was taking things. I didn't want to even hint at it beforehand. I didn't want to tip-off Mr. G. before I proved Seymour was innocent.

I still didn't know if I should tell Seymour. For the next three days I hardly saw him, except at school. He'd actually come up with an idea and was spending a lot of time at it.

I'd been busy too. Besides thinking about Mr. G., I'd been building another rocket. It was a larger one this time—three kitten lengths—and I was building it perfectly and painting it beautifully because I wasn't going to fly it. It was going to sit safely in the middle of my science project, and I was going to put pictures of space around it. It would look great and nothing would go wrong.

"Eureka!"

That was Seymour phoning on Tuesday night.

"You mean you've invented something?" I asked.

He'd already hung up by the time I asked, but ten minutes later the doorbell rang.

"Where's T-Rex, the mad attacker?" he asked.

"He's in the kitchen. He only attacks when I first get home. After that he settles down."

"You know what's wrong, don't you?" asked Seymour.

I hadn't really thought about anything being wrong. Seymour set a box and his backpack down in the middle of the living room and began to unload them.

"What you've got is a very bored cat. You and your parents are away all day. T-Rex gets bored. When you come home, he attacks."

"Cats don't get bored. They sleep."

"They sleep eighty percent of the time. That still leaves twenty percent of the time to be bored."

"He eats for most of that, plus he's got Alaska to play with," I said.

"I know, I know, but he still needs a little more entertainment, living indoors as he does." Seymour grinned. "Besides," he said, "wait until you see what I've built."

It was made of all those building sets parents give their kids at Christmas in order to turn them into architects. Seymour had also used some extra elastic bands, Epsicle sticks and duct tape.

"I call it The Amuze-A-Kitty. I spelled it wrong on purpose to attract attention. That's good advertising. It's a self-entertaining cat toy," said Seymour. "You know how T-Rex loves to chase things. Well—here is a dangly thing for him to bat around, right?"

"Sure," I said. "But we've already got dangly toys at the store."

"This is different," said Seymour. "Hold this open."

I held open the door of a chute. Seymour loaded it with Ping-Pong balls.

"I tried crumpled balls of paper at first, but they were too lumpy and jammed it," he explained. "And I can't use anything too heavy or it might hit him in the head and knock him out. Ping-Pong balls are perfect."

I began to try to figure out how it worked. A connected to B connected to C...? Seymour went in search of T-Rex.

He didn't have to look far. Both T-Rex and Alaska were watching from the kitchen doorway. Cats are snoopy. They wanted to know what was happening.

"Jiggle the string to get his attention, but not too hard," said Seymour. "We want T-Rex to set it off himself."

I gently jiggled the string. In a flash, T-Rex was across the floor and watching the string with bright hunter's eyes. He batted it once. It swung. He batted it twice. It bounced. He batted it a third time.

SMACK SMACK SMACK SMACK SMACK SMACK...

Forty million Ping-Pong balls exploded out of the chute and bounced around the room like crazed popcorn. Both cats disappeared instantly.

Seymour and I stood in the middle of the room staring at each other. I could tell by the way his hairs stood on end and his eyes were wide that he'd been just as surprised as I'd been.

"It's supposed to launch them one at a time!" said Seymour. "It never did that before."

He spent the next hour trying to fix it. The hinged part just wasn't strong enough to be used over and over again.

"There are some hinges at the store," said Seymour. "Do you think your mom and dad would give me a discount on them?"

I looked at Seymour. I still didn't want to tell him about Mom and Dad suspecting him, but I'd finally come up with a plan, and I was definitely going to need his help.

I told him the part I could tell him. I told him about Mr. G. and the shoplifting.

 Chapter 10

We had to catch Mr. G. in the act.

Whenever Mr. G. got off work, he had a routine. He went to the back room to grab his jacket, but he didn't put it on right away. He carried it bunched up under his arm and went to the front to tell Mom he was leaving. After that he walked through the store—sometimes along one aisle, sometimes along another. He left by the back door. His car was always parked across the alley, and he tossed his jacket inside before he climbed in and drove away.

"Whatever he steals, he must wrap it in his jacket. Once it's in the car, he's home free," I explained to Seymour. "We have to be at the back door. We have to bump into him or trip him or grab his jacket...anything to get him to drop what's inside."

"Maybe I could invent some kind of beeper that goes off," said Seymour.

"That's what the security man is trying to sell Mom and Dad. If we prove that it's Mr. G., then they won't have to spend all that money."

And Seymour would be cleared for good. That's what I kept reminding myself because it felt pretty weird to have a plan to trap someone I'd actually liked.

That Thursday, Mr. G. had a later shift than usual. Seymour and I had been at the store about an hour before it got close to the time he was getting off. We'd kept extra busy to avoid talking to him. Seymour had been helping me clean and reorganize the pet supply shelves.

"Are you really, really sure it's Mr. G.?" asked Seymour.

"It has to be," I said. "Who else could it be?"

"What do you think he'll take?" asked Seymour.

"Usually it's something on one of the lower shelves," I said. "Not really low down but not really high up either. He could already have it wrapped in his jacket, but my guess is he actually picks it up on his way out of the store at the end of the day."

Seymour nodded.

"And it's usually on one of the end shelves for some reason."

"Hey," said Seymour, "that lady looks a lot like your gran, except for the knitting bag. Your gran doesn't do ordinary things like knit."

"Soap," I said.

"What?"

"That's what she always buys. A bar of soap."

"Weird," said Seymour. "I think I'll go check out the hinges. I want to see what size might work for my Amuze-A-Kitty."

It would have all been okay if the restaurant man hadn't come in. He needed coffee filters, and the kind he wanted weren't on the shelves. I had to go into the back room to look for more. I thought I'd hear Mr. G. when he came to get his jacket. I guess I was making too much noise shifting boxes to hear, and when I finally found the filters and turned around, Mr. G.'s jacket was gone.

I hurried into the store. I quickly handed the restaurant man the filters and headed off to look up and down the aisles. I didn't want to spook Mr. G., but if I could actually see him wrapping something in his jacket, I knew I wouldn't be so worried about the plan.

It was too late. I'd gone one way and he'd gone another. He was already almost out the back door. I could see his head just passing by the mirrors along the back wall. Seymour should have been there. Where was Seymour?

If I hurried maybe I could barrel out the back door and run into Mr. G. after all. I took off down the aisle.

And that's when someone tripped me.

"Seymour!"

He jumped on top of me and held me down. He had an amazed look on his face.

"It's a knitting bag that steals things. She's invented a knitting bag that steals things!"

"Seymour! Mr. G. is getting away!"

"It's not Mr. G. It's the lady with the frizzy hair. That knitting bag she carries has a trapdoor bottom. She didn't know I was watching. She set it on top of the music box on that end shelf, and when she picked it up, presto—no music box. It was like magic!"

"Where is she?" I asked.

"I don't know," said Seymour. "I was so amazed I had to come and tell you right away."

By the time I convinced Seymour to let me up, we could see her pushing through the outside door. Seymour and I raced down the aisle and out the door after her. She must have begun to move a whole lot faster once she left the store, because she was nowhere that I could see.

"There she is!" said Seymour, pointing to the left.

I caught a glimpse of gray frizzy hair just before she turned the corner.

We chased her. Down the street. Around the corner. We had to stop and look again. There she was, almost an entire block away. A white van pulled up beside her. We yelled and waved and began to run again, but if she heard us, she didn't even hesitate. Right before our eyes the soap lady climbed into the van and sped away.

Seymour and I stood with our mouths open. We hadn't even been able to get a license plate number.

"What's up, you two? Something wrong?"

Mr. G. had driven down the alley and spotted us standing on the street waving our arms around. Mr. G.! He wasn't the thief after all!

I felt a wash of shame. And I felt a wash of complete happiness. I didn't have time for either, however. Seymour and I raced across and jumped into his car.

"Follow that van!" called Seymour.

"The soap lady's the shoplifter," I explained as quickly as I could. "She just climbed into that white van!"

Mr. G. slapped the steering wheel and actually looked pleased.

"Go, go, go!" said Seymour.

"No need," said Mr. G. "I didn't suspect the soap lady, but I definitely thought *he* was way too slick."

Seymour and I looked at each other, bewildered.

"I know that white van," said Mr. G. "It belongs to the salesman who's been trying to sell your mom and dad the security system."

"You mean they know each other?" I asked.

"You bet," said Mr. G. "It's a scam. And I think we've just spoiled their fun."

Chapter 11

"Now let me get this straight," said Gran. "Your mom and dad suspected Seymour of shoplifting. And you, TJ, you suspected Mr. G. of shoplifting."

I'd been just as bad as Mom and Dad. I'd suspected Mr. G. without any real proof.

Luckily Mr. G. hadn't found out about it. And Seymour...don't ask me why, but Seymour's feelings weren't even hurt. He was just totally delighted to have been part of catching a couple of crooks. Mom had still apologized to him and given him all the hinges he needed for the next hundred years. Gran was trying to understand everything.

"But it was an older lady who was stealing things? The one you called the soap lady?" asked Gran.

"She was working with the man who was selling the security systems," nodded Seymour. "The whole thing was a trick to make store owners spend money they didn't need to spend."

"The police arrested them last night at a store on the other end of the city. They were doing the same thing there," I told Gran.

"Talk about sneaky," said Gran, shaking her head in disgust.

"Inventors sometimes do sneaky stuff," said Seymour. "The man who invented the first shopping carts secretly hired people to walk up and down the store and push them like they were regular customers.

"But he wasn't stealing from anyone," Seymour quickly added. "He just wanted people to get used to the idea."

The ear-piercing squawk of feedback on a microphone cut through the air. We were in the gymnasium and it was the end of the science fair day. Mom, Dad and even Mr. G. had taken turns away from the store and dropped by in the morning. Gran had showed up about an hour ago.

The school principal was at the microphone.

"I'd like to begin by congratulating everyone on the most successful science fair we've had at the school for some time. Well done, everyone."

There was applause, of course, and then the principal continued.

"The first award I'd like to present is the Information Award. It's based on how well the student can explain his or her project to others. I'd like to commend our winner this year for a very thorough and enthusiastic knowledge of his subject matter. The winner is Gabe."

Gabe—the kid who hates school! Ms. K. really is a witch. Once Ms. K. had got him to use sports for his science project, he'd gone all out, one hundred and ten percent—isn't that what sports people say?

Gabe hadn't just found out how a speed gun works; he'd also learned how people had first measured speed back when they didn't have regular clocks, let alone stopwatches and speed guns. He'd found out the fastest speed of all sorts of things (including cats, which Seymour and I were resource people for) and made charts comparing them. He'd talked to sports trainers about what types of muscles help people run fast or skate fast or jump high or smack a puck or throw a baseball really hard. And the more he learned, the more he found he liked telling other people about it.

The most amazing part is that when he began to have trouble understanding the science behind it, Mr. Wilson had helped him.

"Mr. Wilson really knows his stuff," Gabe explained. "He didn't do the project for me either. In fact, I think we were wrong about him doing kids' projects for them. He's just had so much experience he knows how to pass it along. I might end up being a science teacher like Mr. Wilson when I'm done being a famous hockey player."

Good grief.

The principal gave out five other awards, but none of them went to our class. That was okay. We'd done way better than we'd expected. Ms. K. had risen to the challenge in her quiet, witchy manner, and we hadn't let her down. For the first time in the history of the school there were great science projects on *both* sides of the gym.

"Let's go look at your invention again, Seymour," said Gran.

The Ping-Pong ball machine looked pretty much the same as it did when Seymour had first brought it over to my house. It worked the same too. Seymour had tried to use the hinges from the store to make it always fire just one ball at a time. Whenever he got one part of it under control, however, something else would give and—*boom*—it would explode balls everywhere. The cats got so they wouldn't go anywhere near the thing.

That's when Seymour had his true brain wave. He decided it wasn't something for cats to play with at all. It was something to keep cats away. He renamed it The Cat-Astrophe and set it by the china cabinet. Alaska hadn't gone anywhere near Mom's special ornaments ever since.

"You know, Seymour, if you don't mind, I think I'll steal your idea next year."

We turned to find Ms. K. and Amanda standing behind us.

"My idea for the Cat-Astrophe machine?" asked Seymour.

"No, no," said Ms. K. quickly. "I mean the idea of inventing something. I'll suggest it to my students next year. I think it's an idea that might really take off. We might even get more awards than Mr. Wilson's class by encouraging students to let their imaginations take flight."

Seymour looked at me meaningfully. So did Amanda. What was going on?

"Take off," said Seymour.

"Take flight," repeated Amanda.

They looked at me. They looked at my rocket. I figured it out. So did Ms. K.

"Does your rocket fly, TJ?" asked Ms. K. "I thought it was just a model."

Gran was smiling, but she didn't say a word.

"It does fly," I said, "but sometimes things go wrong and it flies crooked. Sometimes I forget to put wadding in and the plastic streamers melt."

I'd finally figured out what that black sticky stuff was.

"Would you like to try?" asked Ms. K. "The prizes have already been awarded. You won't be docked if something goes wrong."

It wasn't the prizes I cared about. I looked around the room. Mr. Wilson was talking to Gabe, Mia and some of the other kids in our class. He was actually interested in their projects. Maybe next year, now that he knew he wasn't the only teacher who was good at getting kids enthusiastic about science, he'd share some of his fancy equipment. I didn't want to ruin that for other kids.

And there was something else too. I'd done it. I'd figured out how to play it safe around Mr. Wilson. I'd set up my rocket and then I'd sat in one place beside it.

I'd spent the entire afternoon in the gym without anything going wrong. It was time to quit while I was ahead.

I looked at Ms. K. and shook my head. She nodded and began to talk with Gran about some of the other projects nearby.

That's when I felt it. That sick feeling again. How could I feel sick? Everything had gone great. Everything had gone super.

But at that moment I realized something I hadn't understood before. By playing it safe I wouldn't have to worry about things going wrong, but I'd also lose the chance to do something I *really did want to try.*

"Wait!" I said. "I've changed my mind. I think."

The next moment Seymour and Amanda were helping me pack everything outside before I could change my mind back again.

"Being nervous is okay so long as you use it to do a good job. I'm scared silly every time I try something in front of people," said Amanda.

I didn't know the smartest kid in class got stage fright.

"It's going to work this time, TJ," said Seymour. "I discussed all this with Alaska and T-Rex last night when I was showing them the Cat-Astrophe machine."

Which was ridiculous, but I knew it was Seymour's way of saying he was behind me too.

I went over everything in my head. I knew now that while it was true that model rockets were safe, they were also very finicky. Everything had to be exactly right if you wanted to have a perfect launch, and a perfect launch also meant bringing the rocket back to earth undamaged again.

The body type and engine size had to match. The fins had to be firm and perfectly lined up. The parachute had to be folded properly, not just shoved in. There had to be fireproof wadding between the engine and the streamers or the parachute to keep the heat of the engine from melting the plastic.

It's a good thing I had lots to think about because somehow word had spread and the entire school was now filing onto the side of the playing field to watch.

Gabe was there with his borrowed radar gun to see if he could measure how fast the rocket travelled. Mr. Wilson had hurried down to his laboratory and come back with something that would measure how high it flew. I knew these things were happening because kids were calling across the field, but I tried not to hear. I tried to concentrate on setting up the rocket exactly as it needed to be set up.

At last everything was ready. I nodded to Seymour to begin the countdown.

"Ten, nine..."

His voice was clear and steady on the afternoon air.

"Eight, seven..."

The other kids in our class began to count too.

"Six, five..."

More kids were counting.

"Four, three..."

More and more voices.

"Two..."

It sounded like the entire school.

"One..."

I took a single slow, wonderful breath. The entire school was watching, but the truth is I forgot all about them. It felt like just me and the rocket.

"Blastoff!" called Seymour

FSSSSSSSSSSSSSSS...

It must have been the longest second in history. This was a much larger and heavier rocket, and for two complete heartbeats there was a lot of smoke and sound but no upward motion. It just seemed to sit there on the brink, quivering. Oh no! It really was going to fall apart right on the launchpad!

And then...

Swooo...

ooooo...

oooosh!

It was off! It rose into the air smooth and sleek and eager as if it was born to fly. Up and up and up—sure and strong with a glorious rushing sound both powerful and sweet.

"Yahoo!" shouted Seymour.

The thrust stage was over and momentum alone was carrying it upward against gravity. I could see it slowing. It was wonderfully high in the air.

"One, one thousand. Two, one thousand."

I was counting under my breath. This time it would be five full seconds before the smaller charge would, *I hoped,* pop the nose cone and I'd find out if the launch was really a success.

"Three, one thousand. Four, one thousand."

The rocket had reached maximum height. It seemed to hang in the air.

"Five, one thousa..."

And then it happened. A perfect circle of red and white appeared round and full and beautiful against the blue of the sky.

The parachute had opened.

My brave little rocket was returning safely home.

My name is TJ Barnes—rocket man.

The books where Seymour found his facts about inventions:

Brockman, John (editor). *The Greatest Inventions of the Past 2,000 Years.* New York: Simon and Schuster, 2000.

Caney, Steven. *The Invention Book.* New York: Workman Publishing Co., 1985.

Gardner, Robert. *Experimenting with Inventions.* New York: Franklin Watts, 1990.

Hopper, Meredith. *I for Invention—Stories and Facts about Everyday Inventions.* London: Pan Macmillan Children's Books, 1992.

Jones, Charlotte Foltz. *Mistakes that Worked.* New York: Doubleday, 1991.

Platt, Richard. *The Macmillan Visual Timeline of Inventions.* Toronto: Macmillan Canada, 1994.

Vare, Ethlie Ann and Greg Ptacke. *Patently Female—Stories of Women Inventors and Their Breakthrough Ideas.* New York: John Wiley and Sons, 2002.

Wulffson, Don L. *The Kid Who Invented the Popsicle.* New York: Penguin Putnam, 1997.

Wulffson, Don L. *Toys! Amazing Stories Behind Some Great Inventions.* New York: Henry Holt and Co., 2000.

Hazel Hutchins is a prolific, award-winning author for children who knows how to make her readers laugh and cry while keeping them on the edge of their seats. Hazel was captivated by rockets when her son bought a kit at a garage sale when he was ten. He helped her with the technical details for her story. Hazel lives in Canmore, Alberta.

Canyon School

Date Due

JAN - 3 2005			
APR 17 2008			

BRODART, INC.   Cat. No. 23 233   Printed in U.S.A.